For Sarah

ISBN 0-8109-3733-6

First published in Great Britain in 1994 by
National Trust (Enterprises) Ltd., London

Published in 1994 by Harry N. Abrams, Incorporated, New York
A Times Mirror Company

Designed by Butterworth Design
Production by Bob Towell

Printed and bound in Hong Kong

IAN PENNEY'S ~BOOK OF~ NURSERY RHYMES

ILLUSTRATED BY IAN PENNEY

HARRY N. ABRAMS, INC., PUBLISHERS

This book belongs to

....

Contents

Lavender's Blue

Lavender's blue, dilly, dilly,
Lavender's green;
When I am King, dilly, dilly,
You shall be Queen.

Call up your men, dilly, dilly,
Set them to work,
Some to the plough, dilly, dilly,
Some to the cart.

Some to make hay, dilly, dilly,
Some to thresh corn;
Whilst you and I, dilly, dilly,
Keep ourselves warm.

Hickory, Dickory, Dock

Hickory, dickory, dock,
    The mouse ran up the clock.
The clock struck one,
    The mouse ran down,
Hickory, dickory, dock.

Mary, Mary, Quite Contrary

Mary, Mary, quite contrary,
How does your garden grow?
With silver bells and cockle shells,
And pretty maids all in a row.

There Was A Crooked Man

There was a crooked man
　　Who walked a crooked mile.
He found a crooked sixpence
　　Upon a crooked stile.
He bought a crooked cat
　　Who caught a crooked mouse,
And they all lived together
　　In a little crooked house.

Bobby Shaftoe's Gone to Sea

Bobby Shaftoe's gone to sea,
    Silver buckles on his knee;
When he comes back, he'll marry me,
    Bonny Bobby Shaftoe!

Bobby Shaftoe's bright and fair,
    Combing down his yellow hair;
He's my ain for evermair,
    Bonny Bobby Shaftoe.

B
S

One, Two, Three, Four, Five

One, two, three, four, five,
Once I caught a fish alive,
Six, seven, eight, nine, ten,
Then I put it back again.

Why did you let it go?
Because it bit my finger so.
Which finger did it bite?
This little finger on the right.

Humpty Dumpty

Humpty Dumpty sat on a wall,
Humpty Dumpty had a great fall.
All the King's horses and all the King's men
Couldn't put Humpty together again.

Goosey, Goosey Gander

Goosey, goosey gander,
Whither shall I wander?
Upstairs and downstairs,
And in my lady's chamber.
There I met an old man,
Who would not say his prayers,
I took him by the left leg,
And threw him down the stairs.

Little Bo-Peep

Little Bo-peep has lost her sheep,
And doesn't know where to find them.
Leave them alone, and they'll come home,
Bringing their tails behind them.

Little Bo-peep fell fast asleep,
And dreamt she heard them bleating.
But when she awoke, 'twas all a joke,
For they were still a-fleeting.

Ride a Cock-Horse

Ride a cock-horse to Banbury Cross,
To see a fine lady upon a white horse.
Rings on her fingers and bells on her toes,
She shall have music wherever she goes.

S
P

Oranges And Lemons

"Oranges and Lemons",
Say the bells of St Clement's.
"You owe me five farthings",
Say the bells of St Martin's.
"When will you pay me?"
Say the bells of Old Bailey.
"When I grow rich",
Say the bells of Shoreditch.
"Pray, when will that be?"
Say the bells at Stepney.
"I'm sure I don't know",
Says the great bell at Bow.

Sing A Song Of Sixpence

Sing a song of sixpence,
A pocket full of rye;
Four-and-twenty blackbirds
Baked in a pie.
When the pie was opened,
The birds began to sing;
Wasn't that a dainty dish
To set before the King?

The King was in his counting house
Counting out his money;
The Queen was in the parlour
Eating bread and honey.
The maid was in the garden
Hanging out the clothes;
When down came a blackbird
And pecked off her nose.

4.lb
2.lb

Where Are You Going To?

"Where are you going to, my pretty maid?"
"I'm going a-milking, sir," she said.
"May I go with you, my pretty maid?"
"You're kindly welcome, sir," she said.
"What is your father, my pretty maid?"
"My father's a farmer, sir," she said.
"What is your fortune, my pretty maid?"
"My face is my fortune, sir," she said.
"Then I can't marry you, my pretty maid."
"Nobody asked you, sir," she said.

Little Boy Blue

Little Boy Blue, come blow your horn,
The sheep's in the meadow,
The cow's in the corn.
But where is the boy who looks after the sheep?
He's under a haystack, fast asleep.

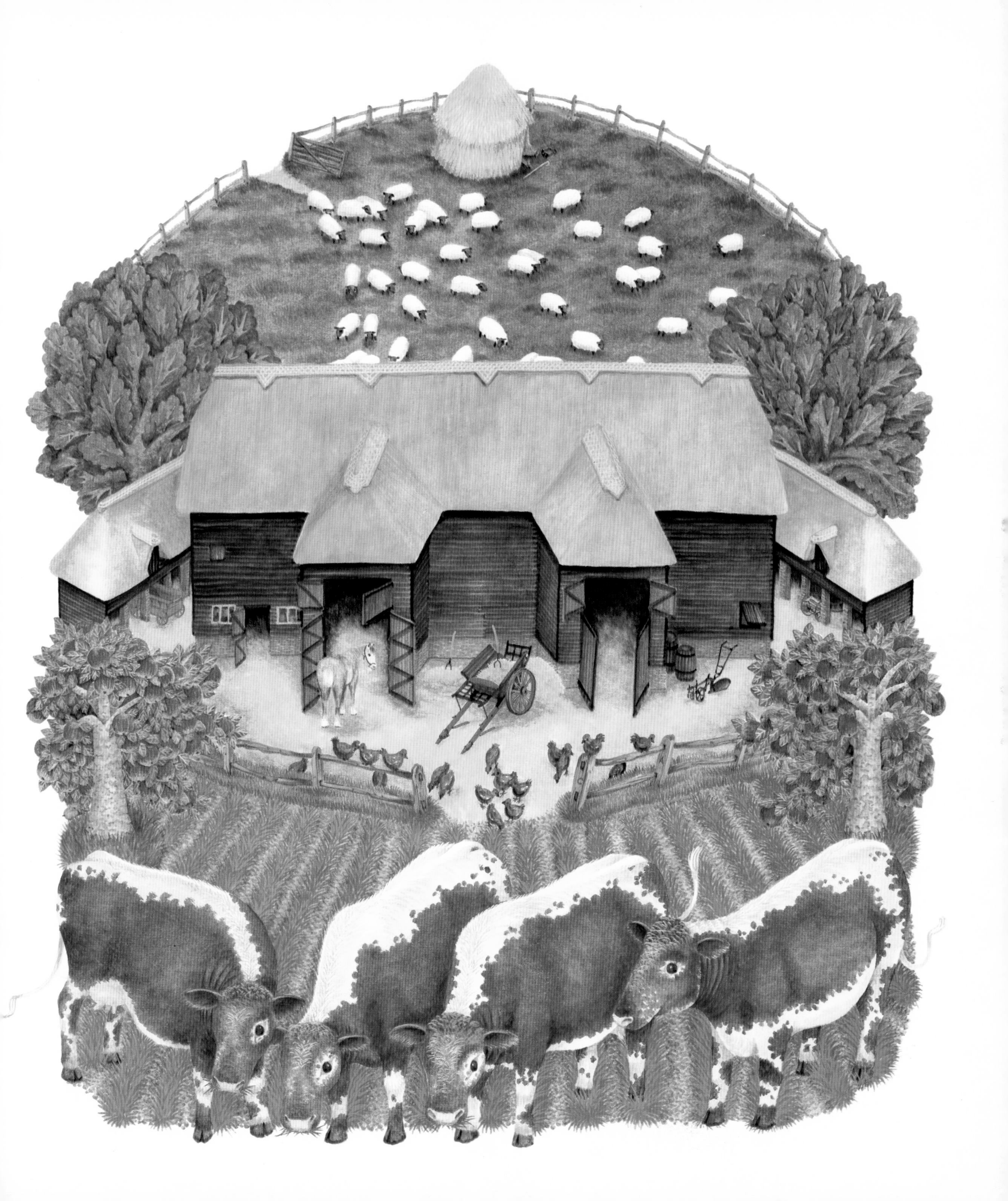

Many of the beloved nursery rhymes
that American children have enjoyed for generations
have their origins in seventeenth-century England.
Ian Penney has therefore appropriately set his
delightful illustrations for the rhymes included here
in actual gardens, houses, and pastures, specifically
those that have been preserved by the National Trust
throughout Great Britain.